HOSPITAL

FARM

Tabby Cat and the Cockerel

This book belongs to...

....

HOSPITAL FARM
Tabby Cat and the Cockerel

Written by Jackie Andrews
Illustrated by Jacqueline East

Bright ☆ Sparks

This is Haven Farm Animal Hospital.

It's a special place for animals in need of care.

Joe and Sally live here, with Mum, Dad,
Patch the dog and Tabby the cat.

Mum runs the farm.

Dad is a vet. He helps the sick animals to get better.

Joe and Sally help with the farm and care for the animals.

Haven Farm is not only a hospital. There are also lots of animals, who live on the farm all the time.

One of these is Tabby the cat. She came to Haven Farm as a stray kitten, a long time ago.

Sally and Joe fell in love with her straight away and Tabby soon became part of the family.

Tabby likes nothing better than to curl up in a sunny, quiet corner of the barn. There she can keep a look out for mice and watch Sally and Joe help Mum around the farm.

But there is one thing that spoils
Tabby's peace and quiet –
Charlie the cockerel.

"Poor Tabby," said Sally one day, as she stroked the cat's head. "She just doesn't like Charlie."

"Well, he is noisy and bossy," said Joe, looking across at the chickens and the cockerel.

Charlie was strutting along the gate, watching Tabby out of the corner of his eye.

"Cock-a-doodle-doo!" he crowed, loudly.

Suddenly, Tabby jumped out of Sally's arms and ran towards the cockerel.

"No, Tabby, no!" shouted Sally.

But, as Tabby leapt up at the cheeky cockerel, Charlie just fluttered into the safety of the hen house, clucking and squawking.

This was a game that Tabby and Charlie had played many times before.

"Missed him again!" laughed Joe.

Tabby just looked cross and walked off to the barn for some peace and quiet.

A few days later, Tabby wasn't really in the mood for Charlie's antics. Her ear was hurting and every time Charlie crowed, it made her feel worse. So, she curled up in her favourite spot and tried to go to sleep.

"Cock-a-doodle-doo!" cried Charlie, suddenly.

Tabby screeched and fled across the farmyard.

Charlie thought how clever he had been to scare Tabby and crowed loudly again.

"Hey, look at Tabby!" cried Joe.

Sally looked up to see Tabby running across the yard, as fast as she could go.

"Something's frightened her," said Joe.

Then, they saw Charlie, looking very pleased with himself.
They knew that he had been up to his old tricks again!

"Come on, Joe," said Sally. "We must find Tabby."

They walked towards the cow shed, where they had last seen her.

"Look!" said Joe. "There she goes."

As they watched, Tabby ran straight up the side of the cow shed and jumped onto the roof.

"Oh, no!" said Sally. "We'll never get her now."

At last, Tabby stopped running. That silly cockerel had really frightened her.

Tabby looked around. The ground looked a *long* way down!

She took a few, careful steps, but suddenly, she felt very dizzy and started to fall.

Tabby landed with a bump! She had slipped off the roof and was now stuck between the cow shed and a wall!

"Miaooow!" she cried.

Joe and Sally ran off to get Dad. They needed his help to rescue Tabby.

"Dad, come quick!" they shouted. "Tabby is in real trouble. She's just fallen off the roof!"

Joe brought a cat carrier and Dad carried a special pole with a loop on the end of it.

Sally looked worried. "That won't hurt her, will it, Dad?" she asked.

"No, she just won't like it very much," said Dad, "but it's the safest way to catch her and pull her free."

Dad squeezed his arm into the gap behind the cow shed.

"I think I need to go on a diet," he joked. "You two had better make sure I don't get stuck as well!"

"Don't worry, Dad," said Joe. "We *would* rescue you."

After a few tries, Dad slipped the loop over Tabby's head and gently pulled her towards him. She was crying and wriggling, as Dad put her into the cat basket.

"Right!" said Dad. "Let's take her to the surgery."

Tabby sat on the examination table, while Dad gently checked her all over.

"Luckily, no bones broken," he said. Joe and Sally sighed with relief.

Then, he used a special instrument to look in Tabby's ears.

"But, she has got a nasty ear infection," he said. "That would have made her dizzy. I'll give her some pills to make her better and we'll keep her indoors for a little while."

"No more Charlie-chasing for you," said Sally, giving Tabby a big cuddle later that day.

"Not yet, anyway," Tabby thought to herself.

She settled down in a comfy armchair, pleased with all the fuss, and was soon fast asleep. She didn't see Charlie peeking in the window, to see if she was all right.

Happy that Tabby was going to be fine, Charlie strutted back to the hen house and *very quietly* crowed... "Cock-a-doodle-doo!"

Being quiet wouldn't be too hard. Well, until Tabby was back to her good old self!

Bright
Sparks

Thank you for buying this Bright Sparks book.

We donate one book to less fortunate children for every two sold.
We have already donated over 150,000 books.

We want to help the world to read.

This is a Bright Sparks book
First published in 2002
Bright Sparks, Queen Street House,
4 Queen Street, BATH BA1 1HE, UK
Copyright © Parragon 2002

Created and produced by
The Complete Works
St Mary's Road,
Royal Leamington Spa,
Warwickshire CV31 1JP, UK

Printed in China
ISBN 1-84250-409-6